MW00745108

PETER the PERSNICKETY

BY BRECKYN WOOD

ILLUSTRATED BY TAIS LEMOS

Cover design by Phillip Colhouer

goodandbeautiful.com

Once upon a time in the Kingdom of Gulp, there lived a prince whose name was Peter.

Prince Peter only ever atc three things: a peanut butter sandwich on brown bread cut into four triangles of the exact same size; twisty noodles with only a little butter but no sauce of any kind; and a red apple with the skin peeled off. If anyone tried to sneak

him a green or yellow apple
with the skin peeled off, as
Cook often did, he would
know with one sniff and
clamp his mouth shut.

Oh, how Cook tried to
tempt him to eat something
else! On shining silver
plates, she brought him
dish after dish—fried eggs
with yolks like a sunrise,

mouthwatering meatballs swimming in sauce, golden toast bubbling with gooey cheese, and perfectly ripe strawberries in blankets of sweet cream. The long table groaned under the weight of these dishes, but Prince Peter only ever pushed the food around on his plate, pretending that tiny peas were brave knights who had to climb Mount Meatball to save Princess Parsnip.

Many royal dinners ended this way, with Peter's mouth shut tight; the queen weeping on bended knee beside him; and the king, red in the face, trying very hard to not jab his fork into the table.

The people of the kingdom began to call him "Peter the Persnickety," which is a fancy word for "picky" or "hard to please." Peter,

of course, thought he was very easy to please, as long as Cook didn't run out of peanut butter.

One day, a traveling salesman from a distant land came to Gulp to sell his famous pies. They were the most delicious thing anyone in the kingdom had ever eaten, and soon

everyone wanted to try one. A guard posted outside the castle gates bought two as the salesman's wagon drove by. After just one bite, he ran into the castle, metal armor clanking. "Your Majesties! Your Majesties!" he shouted through a mouthful of flaky, buttery crust.

The king and queen looked up in surprise. It was not every day that a guard came bursting into the throne room with a pie in each hand.

"What do you think you are doing? Get out of here at once!" hissed the king's advisor.

"I beg pardon, sir, but

the king and queen must try this," said the guard, kneeling and holding up the pie he had not already taken a bite out of. "I ain't never had anything like it. The townsfolk are going mad trying to get their hands on 'em."

"Their Majesties do not want to eat peasant

food out of the hands of
a common guardsman!"
the advisor shouted. He
pointed at the door. "Out!"

"Wait a moment,
Bertram," said the king,
who had caught a whiff
of the pies and was
now looking with great
interest at the guard.
King Roland, it must be

said, did not share his son's dislike of new foods. In fact, his enthusiastic eating habits had earned him the nickname "Roland the Rotund," which is a fancy word for "round" or "plump."

"Bring it here, er—"

"Gregor, Your Majesty," said Gregor, the guard. He

stood up and placed the pie upon the map table, there being no shining silver plates around.

"Roland, dear, I don't think you should—" the queen began.

"Don't fuss, Helena, it's only a pie," said the king, a small piece of it already halfway to his lips. King

Roland chewed for a moment and then, without warning, opened his mouth as wide as it would go and

stuffed the whole rest of
the pie in.

"Gregor!" the king
exclaimed, only it sounded

like "Hmm-hrr!" because his mouth was, of course, very full. Usually it is quite rude to talk with one's mouth full, but this was an especially delicious pie, and besides that, kings often get away with such things.

King Roland swallowed and tried again. "Gregor! Bring me the person who

made this pie and tell him
I will buy his entire stock.
Everyone in the kingdom
shall try them. Quickly!"

That night, the castle
halls rang with sounds of
feasting and merrymaking.
The royal musicians harped,
fluted, drummed, and
trumpeted. Lips smacked,

plates clattered, and the pies kept on coming.

For once, the king and queen were too happy to notice that Peter was not eating but pretending his pie was a poor soldier, captured by the evil Count Cutlery and imprisoned in the Bowl of Doom. No one saw him sneak off to his

room early, munching a peeled apple.

When Peter awoke the next morning, silence had settled over the castle.

Where were the servants who usually opened his curtains and helped him dress? Where was the maid who brought his breakfast apple?

Peter climbed out of bed and dragged open the heavy curtains, thinking it might still be the middle of the night. But the blazing sun of mid-morning struck his sleepy eyes, and what was more . . . there was no one outside. No gardeners, no guards, no mother out for her daily walk among the rosebushes. Peter became perplexed, which is a fancy word for "confused and worried."

Still in his nightshirt,

Peter stepped into the hallway, the stones cold on his bare feet. As he passed room after empty room,

his heart began to pound most unpleasantly. No one in the throne room, no one in the ballroom, no one in the library, no one in the chapel. Peter was running now, his breath fast and ragged, to the last room in the castle.

"Cook!" he gasped as he burst through the kitchen

doors. And there she was, her familiar old face looking so kind in the fire's glow that Peter thought he'd cry.

"Oh, my dear boy, I forgot about you!" she cried, holding out one arm for him to run to while the other kept stoking the fire under a huge black pot. Peter burrowed his face into her side. "Poor chickie," she murmured.

"Where is everyone? What's happened?" asked Peter in muffled tones from Cook's apron.

"'Tis a sad business," she said, shaking her head. "Dunno when I've seen so many folks so sick. That pie man ought to be ashamed o' himself!"

"Sick?" said Peter. "Sick how?"

"Them blasted pies!" Cook roared. "The good king ate enough of 'em to sicken himself for sure, even if there hadn't been something fishy about 'em."

"Fish?" said Peter. "Yuck."

"Not real fish, boy," Cook continued, jabbing angrily at the logs. "Just something nasty that's made the whole kingdom lose their stomachs! Can't keep a thing down besides this broth." She clanged the side of the great pot with her fire poker. "And every one of 'em's covered in purple spots the size o' plums. Has the doctor 'bout ready to tear his hair out."

Peter didn't like plums, and he didn't like the sound of this illness either. "Where are they all now, Cook?"

"Doctor Merek's set up tents by the river. He's got a few helping hands, but not many, and they've been working through the night. They'll need this broth, so be a good lad and take two kettles of it down to the camp," she said, handing him the heavy containers.

Peter heard and smelled the camp before he saw it—a groaning, stinking, miserable place. He staggered from tent to tent in search of the

doctor, passing rows of the sick with their sweaty, purple-spotted faces. His throat squeezed tight.

"You there, boy! Bring me those kettles," the doctor

called from the next tent
over.

As Peter approached, the
doctor's eyebrows jumped.
"Your Highness! Goodness
me. I didn't realize . . . But
of course you'd be safe
from all this."

Peter and the doctor
began pouring bowls of
broth and handing them

around to the sick. "Merek," Peter said, his voice wobbly, "everyone will be all right, won't they? And my parents, how are they?"

The doctor sighed. "The king and queen are in a bad way, but they're strong. They'll pull through. Wish I could say the same for everyone. I don't know . . ."

Peter patted one little girl on a cot. She looked so sad. "What can I do, Merek?" Peter asked. "I am the prince," he said, standing a little taller. "It is my job to take care of the kingdom while my parents are sick."

The doctor gave Peter a searching look. "We are in a pickle," he began.

"I don't like pickles," said Peter.

"Right. I mean we're in trouble. But there is something that might help."

"What is it?" Peter asked. Merek finished wiping broth from one man's chin and handed the cloth to a worker. "Come with me."

The doctor led Peter to a table piled with dusty books. "I've been using every spare moment to search through my books for a possible cure, and I think I've found it." He pointed to an open page that had drawings of different plants. "There is a bush whose leaves were

once used to cure stomach
diseases and 'painful spots
upon the skin.' Someone
needs to go into the forest,
perhaps very deep in, find

the right bush, and bring back as many of its leaves as possible."

"I can do that!" Peter smiled. "I have been hunting in the woods many times with my father. I am not afraid."

Merek looked relieved. "Bless you, Your Highness. I must stay here and do what

I can for these people. And the few helpers I have are field workers; they cannot read, at least, not very well. You must take this as a guide. It will help you find the right plant." He held the book out to Peter. "Bring back as much as you can as quickly as you can."

"I will do my best, Merek,"

Peter promised.

"You're a good egg, Peter,"
Merek said, patting the
prince's shoulder.

Peter made a face.

"I know, I know," the
doctor sighed. "You don't
like eggs."

Although Peter was, of
course, saddened and

worried about the terrible
illness, it was not without
some excitement that he
entered the forest that day.
This was, after all, very
much like a quest, and all
the princes he had read
about were always going
on quests, with swords
blazing and banners flying.
Peter was ready to climb

mountains, ford raging rivers, and fight deadly foes. Unfortunately, after

about an hour's walk into the forest, Peter had encountered none of these, so he sat down on a stump to consult the doctor's book.

"It says here I must find a bush whose leaves have three points of equal size," Peter spoke aloud to himself. "That shouldn't be too hard."

He began to search the bushes along the path, but these all had round leaves with no point. He found heart-shaped leaves and leaves with two points and leaves with four. Once, his sleeve caught on a thorn and ripped, and soon after he tripped over a tree root.

Brushing the dirt from

his hands, Peter again opened the book, hoping for further guidance. "This particular bush is often found along the banks of rivers and lakes," he read. This information would, of course, have been helpful to know before Peter began crashing through the underbrush, but a quest is nothing if not a learning experience for its hero, so we will forgive Peter for not yet realizing that he ought to read the whole page before continuing on.

Peter knew of a fishing stream deeper in the forest, and it was for this stream that he now headed. The sun was beating down quite hot, and the thick book became heavier with each step. The prince's stomach began to grumble, too, and he realized he had not brought any food, not one peanut butter sandwich. This quest was turning out to be much less glamorous than Peter had hoped, which is a fancy word for "exciting" or "charming." An hour or so more of walking and Peter found

the stream. Had he not
been persnickety about
such things, he would
have plunged into its cool

depths and taken several long gulps. Instead, he sipped the warm water from his flask, which is an old-fashioned sort of water bottle, and soaked his tired feet in the stream. On the far side of the bank, Peter spotted a bush that looked promising, so he balanced the book on top of his head and waded across the waist-deep stream.

But alas, it was not the right sort of bush, and Peter kicked it in frustration, receiving only a stubbed toe for his efforts. He sat down in a huff and again opened the book.

"It grows only along northern banks," he read.

Peter groaned and waded back across to the north side of the stream.

 After another hour searching along the northern bank, Peter let out a cry at the sight of a three-pointed leaf, swaying in the breeze. This was it, at last! A fat, lovely bush full of the little things. And

next to it, another, and
another—a long line of
them stretching beyond his
sight. Peter was exultant,

57

which is a fancy word for "very happy," and began ripping leaves off and stuffing them into his bag. But the day's events having had some effect, Peter stopped and checked the book once more, to see if it had any advice on picking the leaves.

And there, at the very

bottom of the page, were words that made Peter's heart stop.

"Beware of false copies of this plant, which are bitter in taste and will not make

the medicine. The true plant bears sweet leaves."

Peter looked from the leaves in his hands to the drawings on the page. They were the same—three long points of equal size. Surely it was the right plant? Surely there would be no need to . . . to . . .

He tore a leaf in half and

held it to his nose, trying to detect a hint of sweetness.

Nothing.

A sweat broke out on his forehead, though the sun had gone behind a cloud.

The prince poked the tip of his tongue between his lips and brushed the leaf across it quickly.

Still nothing.

Every quest must end with a battle, and this was Peter's. He would rather have fought an army, wrestled a lion, or

swam across a moat full of crocodiles, but those things wouldn't save the people of Gulp. Screwing his eyes shut tight and picturing

the poor faces of the sick at home, Prince Peter the Persnickety opened his mouth wide and shoved the leaf inside. After a few chews, a bitter taste filled his mouth, and he spat.

Amazed at his own daring, he moved to the next bush and tried again, and then the next, and then the next, spitting out each bitter leaf. After ten bushes, he gargled with some water from his flask and tried ten more. At the twenty-first bush, Peter tasted a sweetness that seemed to sing.

He fell to the ground and slept with a smile on his face.

Our triumphant prince returned to the castle the next morning dirty, sore, and absolutely ravenous, which is a fancy word for "very hungry." After handing his bulging bag over to the doctor, he fell upon a plate of beef and cheese rolls Cook had brought out for the workers.

Peter the Persnickety

Cook's eyes popped. "Someone has left my Peter in the woods and sent home this hungry bear in his place!" she cried.

Peter smiled with cheeks full of beef. "This bear wouldn't mind some of your best honey cakes, dearest Cook."

The old woman laughed

a belly-shaking laugh and turned to walk back to the kitchen.

The tea made from Peter's leaves quickly restored everyone in the kingdom to good health, but it took a bit longer to restore their appetites.

One night a few weeks after the prince's quest,

Cook made a lovely chicken and ham tart, which is just a fancy word for "pie." Peter ate it eagerly and asked for seconds, but the king and queen sat there getting purple in the face.

"Cook?" said the king, holding his hand to his stomach. "Could I have a peanut butter sandwich?"

The End

Try a Level 3 Book from
The Good and the Beautiful Library*

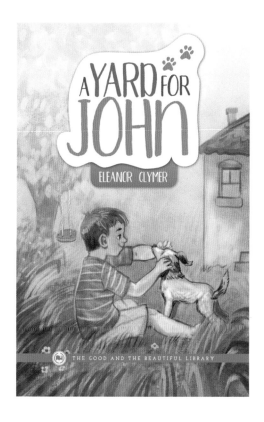

*Reading level assessment is available at
goodandbeautiful.com*

Printed in China